Louisa May &
Mr. Thoreau's Flute

Julie Dunlap *&* Marybeth Lorbiecki
Pictures by **Mary Azarian**

Dial Books for Young Readers
NEW YORK

For my little Louisas, Hannah and Sarah J.D.

And mine, Nadja and Mirjana M.L.

For Peg and Audrey—may you always be free spirits M.A.

Published by Dial Books for Young Readers
A division of Penguin Putnam Inc.
345 Hudson Street • New York, New York 10014
Text copyright © 2002 by Julie Dunlap and Marybeth Lorbiecki
Pictures copyright © 2002 by Mary Azarian
All rights reserved • Designed by Nancy R. Leo-Kelly
Text set in Monotype Bell
Printed in Hong Kong on acid-free paper
1 3 5 7 9 10 8 6 4 2

Library of Congress Cataloging-in-Publication Data
Dunlap, Julie.
Louisa May and Mr. Thoreau's flute / by Julie Dunlap
and Marybeth Lorbiecki; pictures by Mary Azarian.
p. cm.
Summary: In nineteenth-century Concord, Massachusetts, seven-year-old Louisa May Alcott
joins other local children on the varied excursions led by teacher and naturalist
Henry David Thoreau, and is inspired to write her first poem.
ISBN 0-8037-2470-5
1. Alcott, Louisa May, 1832–1888—Childhood and youth—Juvenile fiction.
[1. Alcott, Louisa May, 1832–1888—Childhood and youth—Fiction.
2. Thoreau, Henry David, 1817–1862—Fiction. 3. Authors, American—Fiction.
4. Writing—Fiction. 5. Concord (Mass.)—Fiction.]
I. Lorbiecki, Marybeth. II. Azarian, Mary, ill. III. Title.
PZ7.L8766 Lo 2002   [Fic]—dc21   00-059043

The illustrations are woodcuts, hand-colored with acrylic paints.

<u>Note</u>

The basic facts within this story are true, with details gathered from journals, letters, and other writings of Louisa May Alcott, Henry David Thoreau, and their families and friends. But parts of the historical record concerning Louisa's friendship with Henry Thoreau are contradictory or incomplete. When sources disagree, we have relied on Madeleine R. Stern's classic biography, *Louisa May Alcott* (University of Oklahoma Press, 1950), and on our understanding of Louisa Alcott's bold, creative spirit.

❧ *Prologue* ❧

Louisa May Alcott is best known for writing the book *Little Women*, the ever-popular story about four girls growing up during the American Civil War. But as a child, "Louy" Alcott didn't like to write—at least, not the way her father wanted her to.

Her father, Bronson Alcott, was a thinker and teacher with unusual ideas. For a few years, he ran a school in Boston, Massachusetts. But his students' parents came to disapprove of some of his teachings, and eventually the school closed.

So the Alcotts moved to a cottage in the nearby town of Concord, arriving April 1, 1840. They hoped to live off what they could grow and what Mr. Alcott could earn from his writings and speeches (about his unusual ideas). It wasn't easy.

One of their Concord neighbors was Henry David Thoreau. He would later write a famous book called *Walden* about the years he lived alone in the woods, seeking a simple life that didn't depend on money. But in 1840, people didn't think of Thoreau as a writer. They did think he was unusual. Henry Thoreau was a young man, not long out of college, yet he had already traveled a bit, helped with the family pencil business, and lost a good job at the town's school for refusing to whip his pupils.

When the Alcotts arrived in Concord, Henry Thoreau was trying to earn his living again as a teacher, running a new school with his brother, John. He spent his free time wandering the woods and fields, and often welcomed local children along on his expeditions.

This is the story of what Louisa May Alcott discovered on these outings with Mr. Thoreau—about the woods, about writing, and about herself.

"Jump, I dare you!" Cyrus Hosmer taunted.

Seven-year-old Louisa May Alcott peered down from the ceiling beam. The barn floor seemed as far away as heaven, and at least as hard to get to.

"You'll be hurt!" cried her older sister, Anna. "What will Father say?"

Louy already knew. But she saw her new friends the Hosmers grinning, doubting her courage.

She took a deep breath—and leapt.

❦ ❦ ❦

Luckily, Louisa ended up with only two sprained ankles—and piles of lessons for punishment.

Louy lay by the window in Father's study, printing long lists of things good girls do: *speak softly, obey parents, follow rules.* Her fingers throbbed, her head ached, and her quill dribbled more ink blots than words.

Behind her, she heard heavy footsteps. It was Father. "How will I ever tame my wild Louisa?"

She sat up. "Here, Father," she said, showing him the blotched paper.

He sighed, and leaning down, he soothed, "Louisa, writing is not easy. Nor is living a good life. But both are worth the effort."

This did not comfort Louy at all. Then Father told her to write some more! About duty and conscience and trying to be perfect—*his* favorite subjects.

Louy bent back over her paper, trying not to cry. She wished she could please her father. But she feared she'd never be able to write like him—or follow his rules up to heaven.

One sunny Saturday after Louisa's ankles had healed, the Hosmers came banging on the Alcotts' door. "Mr. Thoreau is collecting children for a huckleberry party!" they announced. Louisa sprang up so fast, she dropped her mending.

Mr. Henry David Thoreau was Anna's teacher at the Concord Academy. Louy itched to meet him. Neighbors gossiped that the young teacher was a dreamer and a loafer, the only college man around who didn't wear store-bought clothes. Some even said he combed his hair with a pine cone. But everyone agreed—he knew the best berry patches around.

"Mother, may we go?" Louy pleaded.

Mrs. Alcott hesitated.

"Say yes, Mother," Louy begged. Even proper Anna added a quiet "Please."

Mrs. Alcott glanced at the mending pile, then at her daughters' faces. "Oh, go ahead, girls. We'll surprise your father with a huckleberry pie."

What luck! A chore-free afternoon!

Tin pails in hand, the girls scrambled for seats in the crowded hay rigging. Louy couldn't resist spying on the driver.

Mr. Thoreau's hair does stick out like a prickle bush, Louisa thought, smiling to herself. And his trousers are made of homespun, drab as rabbit fur. But no one had told her about the wooden flute sticking out of his pocket, or the pencil stuck in his hat, or that he hardly had a word for anyone.

But what does it matter? thought Louisa as she laughed and shouted with her friends. At least he's not telling us "Hush!"

The wagon creaked to a stop in a thick woodland. The children tumbled out and hurried down the footpath, following Mr. Thoreau.

Suddenly the line stopped. One of the boys had forgotten his pail.

"Don't fuss over it," Mr. Thoreau gruffed. With a jackknife pulled from nowhere, he cut neat slits in a birch tree and stripped off some bark. Before anyone could ask his plan, he had folded and tucked it into the tidiest berry box Louy had ever seen.

What else could this Mr. Thoreau do?

Louisa and the others pressed forward, but Mr. Thoreau kept stopping along the way. He'd stoop to examine some moss or a wildflower. He'd cup a toad in his hands for all to admire.

When he pulled out a notebook, Louy grimaced. She worried they'd *never* taste huckleberries if Mr. Thoreau started writing. It took her forever to write anything! And Father spent hours scratching out words and trying new ones to craft a perfect sentence.

Mr. Thoreau's notebook disappeared after a few quick jottings.
What could he have written so quickly? Louy wanted to know,
but she had little time to wonder. The berry pickers were off again,
over a hill and straight toward the huckleberries.

Everyone raced for the best picking spots, and Mr. Thoreau exclaimed into the air, "Nothing's more refreshing than wild fruit. A gift from nature for anyone who knows where to look."

"Free fruit!" Louisa cheered. Any food that came without weeding or cooking tasted doubly good to Louisa.

Almost unnoticed, a light melody began to swirl around the huckleberry patch. It seemed to spill from the rocks above.

Looking up from her pail, Louy spotted Mr. Thoreau breathing into his flute.

How could such sweet music come from such a strange man?

Louy closed her eyes and dreamed of a world as rich and bright as the music. Too soon, Mr. Thoreau stopped playing. The thumps and bumps of the wagon ride home jolted the tune out of her head.

Summer faded, and harvesting and pickling were added to the Alcott girls' other duties. There were also diapers to launder and little Lizzy and Baby May to watch.

While Anna worked all day without complaining, Louisa fumed. She tried whistling Mr. Thoreau's tune but her lips just sputtered. Once, she slammed down her broom and shouted, "I'm going outside!"

"Lower your voice," Mother scolded. "And remember your duties."

Quieted, Louisa swept the floor near the doorway—opening it a slit to taste the breeze.

Just when Louy felt she could stand her days no longer, fresh news came from Anna about Mr. Thoreau. He would be taking his students on Saturday field trips. Neighborhood children were welcome to come along.

That one day a week Louy stitched like lightning so Mother would let her go.

Mr. Thoreau led treks to Fair Haven Cliffs, Nut Meadow Brook, and Walden Pond. Some children had trouble keeping pace with his swinging stride. Not Louy.

She didn't want to miss a single one of the teacher's odd lessons. Louy watched, wide-eyed, when Mr. Thoreau's low whistle charmed titlarks from the treetops.

She gasped when, after a tale of the Algonquin Indians, Mr. Thoreau picked up an arrowhead at his feet that no one else had noticed.

And Louisa thrilled to every word of Mr. Thoreau's stories about elves dancing on toadstools. One time she nearly stepped on a cobweb, and he gently caught her arm. "Careful, Louisa. That's a lace handkerchief dropped by a fairy."

Does he write such magical tales in his notebook? Louy hoped so.

Later, as she lay in the pine needles listening to the song of his flute, Louisa pictured fairies peeking out from everywhere.

As days crisped in October, Father insisted, "There won't be time for nonsense." Louisa feared "no nonsense" meant no Saturdays with Mr. Thoreau. Panicked, she turned to her mother. "We'll see, Louisa," was all Mother would promise.

"We'll see" was not good enough. Louisa missed outing after outing. Each time, she felt like she'd missed a trip to a world she might never get another chance to see.

❧ ❧ ❧

One misty Saturday, Mr. Thoreau was leading a trip on the Concord River. The Hosmers couldn't go. Anna knew she shouldn't. But Louisa had to. She just didn't know how.

Father left early to help a neighbor harvest apples. Louisa scrubbed the pots and watched for her chance.

Finally, Mother went to put the baby down for a nap.

Louisa was ready.

"Anna," she called, grabbing her coat, "tell Mother I've gone with Mr. Thoreau."

Before Anna could shout "Wait!" Louy had shot out the door.

She made it to the dock just in time. Mr. Thoreau and a neighbor boy were already untying the boat.

Mr. Thoreau greeted her with a curt nod. "I thought you'd brave the cold to come." Then he tucked a buffalo robe around his two passengers and bent into the oars.

The boat slipped into the current between the wooded banks. Mr. Thoreau let it drift and reached for his flute. A mournful sea chantey mingled with the *shhhhhh* of the breeze.

Louy's mind flowed with the music for miles down the river.

Mr. Thoreau glanced her way. Louy must have had a faraway look in her eyes, for he stopped playing. "The river can take you places, Louisa," he said. "My brother and I rowed for days down this river and north up the Merrimack until we reached the New Hampshire wilderness. That fresh, green land is everything I dreamed. As deep and trackless as the sky."

"Tell me more," Louy urged.

Mr. Thoreau shook his head. "Someday I'll be ready to put it all into words. But not yet. Not yet." He picked up his flute and played on.

Louisa hummed along, trying to hold the tune in her mind.

All the way home from the river, Louy worried about her punishment.

Her mother met her at the door. Louisa froze.

But Mrs. Alcott surprised her with merely a frown. "Just this once," she said, handing Anna's dishrag to Louisa.

Then Mother sent Anna out to play.

❧ ❧ ❧

None of the Alcotts played much the rest of that fall and winter. For Louy's November birthday party, Mrs. Alcott could only afford to serve thin bread squares and apple slices. Father's writing paid nothing, so he chopped wood for a dollar a day. Mother took in sewing to earn a few more pennies. That left Louisa and Anna to mind the house and the other girls.

Sometimes neighbors visited, and they often whispered about Mr. Thoreau. One reported, "He's studying fish under pond ice and chasing foxes through the snow!"

Mr. Alcott scoffed, "Has he nothing better to do?"

Louisa couldn't imagine there *was* anything better.

She slipped away from the chatter and chores to Father's study. Sitting at his desk, Louisa wondered: What would Mr. Thoreau do if he were boxed inside? She could see him playing his music or scribbling away.

But she had no flute. And there was nothing to write about. Only endless tasks and doing your duty. And being stuck in a winter-cold house with three sisters.

Words seemed trapped inside her, like fish under ice.

Through the long, cooped-up days, Louy toiled in the house, struggling to be good but longing for the woods.

Through the long, chilled nights, she hid under heaps of quilts and tried to hum to herself the song from the river. But she couldn't get it right.

❧ ❧ ❧

One March morning, very early, her sleep was shattered with a BOOM! That sound meant one thing—the ice was cracking on the Concord River. Spring!

Breakfast chores could wait. Louy threw off her covers and burst from the cottage.

Concord was alive with sound. Icicles dripped into puddles. A rooster squawked at the long-lost sun. And right in Father's garden, a robin caroled his first song—a twirling melody: *cheerily, cheerup, cheerily.*

Louy felt like singing too. If only she could play the flute like Mr. Thoreau!

Suddenly, words rushed into Louisa's head. Flowing, musical lines about all she saw and heard and felt.

Louisa rushed indoors. She picked up her quill and wrote it all down as it came to her, playing with rhythms and rhymes, choosing some words and crossing out others. Just like Father.

Her first poem!

She couldn't wait to show it to her parents and to Mr. Thoreau! It seemed as beautiful as the notes from Mr. Thoreau's flute. And writing it thrilled her, made her feel powerful and free—like biting into wild huckleberries or leaping from a ceiling beam.

Eight-year-old Louisa May Alcott had discovered her own inner music—a wild, melodious river of words that could carry her wherever she longed to be.

To the First Robin

Welcome, welcome, little stranger,
Fear no harm, and fear no danger;
We are glad to see you here,
For you sing "Sweet Spring is near."

Now the white snow melts away;
Now the flowers blossom gay;
Come dear bird and build your nest,
For we love our robin best.

❧ *Afterword* ❧

When Louisa showed the poem to her mother, the proud Abby Alcott exclaimed, "You will grow up a Shakespeare!"

Louisa's writing bloomed under her parents' supervision. She began a journal two years later, and both parents wrote messages inside as a way to reform her character. Yet Louisa continued to slip away from home to delight in nature's wilds.

At twelve Louisa wrote to a friend that she felt closest to God in the Concord woods. Henry Thoreau had built a hut in these woods, by Walden Pond, and had begun writing about his journey on the Concord and Merrimack rivers. Louisa and her sisters visited him often, picnicking and rowing on the pond.

No one knows if Louisa showed her first poem to Mr. Thoreau, but her first published book was a collection of woodland fairy stories, *Flower Fables*. Eventually Louisa was selling enough of her writing to support her family. In her most famous book, *Little Women*, she created a family much like her own—four girls trying to grow up to be both good daughters and true to themselves. The character inspired by Louy is easy to spot—the free-spirited, headstrong writer Jo March.

Louisa resided in Concord on and off for the rest of her life. Henry Thoreau lived nearby and published his masterpiece, *Walden*, in 1854. He died of tuberculosis on May 6, 1862.

In tribute Louisa composed a poem called "Thoreau's Flute," in which she mourns that "The Genius of the wood is lost." Nature then comforts her by "writing his name in violets" and counseling: "'Seek not for him—he is with thee.'"